Fairy Tales

D1639151

Faber
Stories

Marianne Moore was born in Kirkwood, Missouri, in 1887. She attended Bryn Mawr College, and lived her adult life in New York City, in Manhattan and Brooklyn. She was the author of numerous books of poems, including most notably *Observations* (1924), *Selected Poems* (1935), *The Pangolin and Other Verse* (1936), *What Are Years* (1941), and *Collected Poems* (1951). Her lifelong practice of a radically innovative formal verse, committed to moral courage and spiritual clarity, won her most of the major poetry awards available to an American: the Bollingen Award (1952), the National Book Award (1952), the Pulitzer Prize (1952), the American Academy of Arts and Letters Gold Medal (1953), the Robert Frost Medal from the Poetry Society of America (1967), and the National Medal for Literature (1968). She died on 5 February 1972.

Marianne
Moore

Fairy Tales

Faber
Stories

ff

First published as *Fairy Tales* in 2019
by Faber & Faber Limited
Bloomsbury House
74–77 Great Russell Street
London WC1B 3DA
First published by The Macmillan Company in 1963

Typeset by Faber & Faber Limited
Printed and bound by CPI Group (UK) Ltd, Croydon, CR0 4YY

A CIP record for this book
is available from the British Library

ISBN 978–0–571–35614–0

10 9 8 7 6 5 4 3 2 1

Preface

When I read only a few words of *Puss in Boots,
Cinderella* or some other story by Perrault (pro-
nounced pair-*row*), I cannot stop, but go on to the
very end even though I may have read the story a
few days before (like the poet La Fontaine, who
said about these stories: on hearing two or three
first words, "I am enraptured, really am").

Why am I so interested? One reason is, I think,
that I like names, and the title of a story by Perrault
usually is the name of the principal character—
hero or heroine. I am curious. If the story is named
for someone, the person must have done something
interesting. The master of Puss in Boots is poor, but
again and again Puss finds some way of outwitting
poverty for his master and for himself. He waits
with his sack, then traps a rabbit; we see what he
does and feel what he feels. We wonder what he
will do next.

When we like what we are reading so much that we do not wish to be interrupted or answer a question—when holding our thoughts from being scattered—we win a victory for the mind, Mr. Padraic Colum says. And having seen a problem solved—something begun and completed—the story has done something more for us than interest us, he says; it has left "a pattern of order" in the mind.

In the story of the Sleeping Beauty, the Prince must go through the hedge of thorns if he is to reach the castle and see what is there. "He starts"; "he sees"; "he is all on fire." The words are not just accidental. After Perrault first wrote the stories, he saw ways of making them better. At first he said "the cat" (*le chat* in French) pretended that his master, when almost drowning, had been robbed of his clothes (then Puss could beg the King for others). Since Puss had hid the clothes himself, Perrault changes "cat" to "this rascal" (*ce drôle*; spelled it *drôsle*: either way means a rascal who plays pranks).

When the Sleeping Beauty has married the Prince, she is left in her castle until the Prince prepares a fine welcome for her at Court. Perrault said at first, "She entered the town": that is all. Then, before the words had been printed, he improved them, wrote, "She entered the capital in splendor—one of her children on her left, the other on her right."

Another improvement: In the manuscript of *Cinderella* (the original copy in handwriting), he said, "She had to eat in the kitchen," but did not say why she found life dreary; then made it clear, said, "She was gentle yet was given the hardest, most despised tasks, had to drudge from morning till night, and afterward sleep on straw in an attic." We do not see her face—just what she does (her "actions"), and this helps us to imagine how she looked.

Leaving something to the imagination is one of Perrault's arts. In his telling of *The Sleeping Beauty*, the Prince does *not* wake the Princess with a kiss. The more the Prince cared, Perrault felt, the less willing he could be to intrude.

*

Puss in Boots, The Sleeping Beauty, Cinderella, and other tales of his, Perrault called *Stories of Mother Goose.* The author of the stories was Charles Perrault or his son, Pierre; we have reason—several reasons—to think it was Charles. They were written to amuse Elisabeth Charlotte d'Orléans, the young niece of a French king, Louis XIV. The cover of her handwritten copy was of red leather (morocco) stamped with the "arms" of Elisabeth in gold on the front and on the back. One's coat-of-arms tells something about one in small form. Since Elisabeth Charlotte d'Orléans was of the nobility and the lily is the special flower of France, there are lilies in Elisabeth Charlotte's coat-of-arms: two lilies side by side and one under them, below a crown on the upper rim of which there are lilies all the way round. (According to legend, the lily came to mean "France and royalty" as follows: A very old hermit saw light streaming into his cell one night; then an angel appeared, holding a shield of wonderful beauty; it was sky blue—azure—and on it were three gold lilies that shone like stars. The hermit

4

was commanded by the angel to give the shield to Queen Clotilde. She gave it to King Clovis, her husband; and after that, his soldiers were always victorious.)

The red book stamped with Elisabeth Charlotte's gold lilies was discovered in 1953 in Nice, France, and is now in the Pierpont Morgan Library in New York. *The Sleeping Beauty,* written first, had been printed in 1696 in a magazine called *Le Mercure Galant* (*The Dashing Hermes,* I translate it), and all nine of Perrault's stories were published in one volume the following year.

Dr. Jacques Barchilon, who has translated Perrault, says (I like this very much), "In a fairy tale or fantasy, things happen 'naturally'—marvelous things." "The magical is interwoven with everyday things" of life as we live it day by day.

Marianne Moore

For reading these stories by Perrault to obviate misreadings and oversights by me—assistance without which I would have felt it effrontery to offer the text—I thank Dr. Floyd Zulli, Professor of Romance Languages at New York University: or for giving what one needs most for oneself—*time*—amid academic preoccupations at a season when one does not digress.

Without Mr. Michael Di Capua's resourcefulness, sense of coherence, enthusiasm and intuitiveness, could there have been any Perrault by me to read?

M.M.

December 1962

Puss in Boots

A miller had nothing to leave his three children but his mill, his ass, and his cat. Deciding what to give each was quick work: there was no need of a steward or man with a great seal to make portions legal. That would have eaten up all the poor man had to leave.

The oldest son got the mill; the second, the ass; and the youngest—just the cat. He was dejected that he had such a poor share.

"My brothers," he said, "can make a decent living, helping each other; but I! Once I've eaten him and made his fur into a muff, I've nothing."

The cat, who had heard it all, did not behave as if he had, and said with a businesslike air: "Don't take it so hard, Master; all you have to do is have a pair of boots made for me, so my paws won't be scratched by the brambles, and you will see that you are not so badly off as you think."

The cat's master did not half believe what the cat had said, but many a time had seen what a knack he had in catching rats and mice—how he would hang by his hind paws or bury himself in flour and play dead. Perhaps the case was not hopeless—with no one to rescue him but his cat. He then brought out what had been asked for. Puss drew the boots on like a general, hung a sack around his neck—his front paws holding the strings—and off he went into a brambly place dotted with rabbits. He put roughage and a few straws in the bag, lay flattened out as if dead, and waited for some unwary little rabbit, new to the wiles of the world, to forage in the bag for what was there.

He had scarcely begun to play dead when his hopes were realized; a little dunce of a rabbit crept into the bag; Puss drew the strings up tight, had the rabbit and killed him without a qualm.

Delighted with his prowess, he hastened to the palace and said he must see the King.

Shown up a staircase to the part of the palace reserved for the King, he made a deep bow upon entering, and said, "A wild rabbit, Sire, which the Marquis of Carabas (a name he had invented for his master) wished me to present to you on his behalf."

"Tell your master," replied the King, "that I thank him and am much pleased with his gift."

Another time, Puss hid in a wheatfield—keeping the mouth of the sack open all the time—and when two partridges stepped in, he tightened the drawing-strings and had both, then offered them to the King as he had offered the rabbit. The King was pleased to accept them and presented Puss with a bit of money.

Keeping on in this way for two or three months, Puss took game to the King from time to time as gifts from the Marquis, his master.

Then one day, having heard that the King and his daughter—the loveliest princess in the world—would be out for an airing by the river, he said to his master: "Do as I say and your fortune is made. All you have to do is be bathing in the river at the exact spot I point out, and leave the rest to me."

The Marquis of Carabas obeyed Puss, with no

idea that any particular good was to come of it, and was carelessly enjoying a dip when of a sudden the King was seen approaching. Puss shrilled out in his most piercing tones: "Help! Help! Look—Monsieur, the Marquis of Carabas—drowning!"

Startled, the King turned to look through the pane on his side of the coach, recognized Puss, who had brought him presents of game so many times, had his men-at-arms run to the aid of the Marquis of Carabas; and while they were helping the bedraggled Marquis ashore, Puss came up to the coach, explaining to the King that while his master was in the water, thieves had carried off his clothes—his master having protested with all his might, though in vain.

The rascal had hidden them under a big stone.

The King had the Keeper of his wardrobe select from the many garments in his care one of the handsomest for Monsieur, the Marquis of Carabas, making graceful acknowledgments, meanwhile, of the many favors received.

When the rich attire presented to the miller's son

brought out his good looks (for he was a handsome, well set-up youth), the King's daughter found him much to her liking. The young man, for his part, had never seen a more beautiful princess, and the two had barely exchanged glances when each fell in love with the other.

Rumor does not say if the King noticed; but he had the Marquis step up into the coach and share the rest of the excursion.

Puss, in raptures that his plot was unfolding as he had hoped, ran ahead and, to any farm hands he saw mowing, said: "Good folk, unless you tell the King that the field you are mowing belongs to the Marquis of Carabas, I will have you ground up finer than meat for a *pâté*."

The King did not fail to ask the reapers to whom the meadow belonged.

"To Monsieur, the Marquis of Carabas," they said as one man, for the warning from Puss had left them aquiver with fear.

"You have noble estates," the King said to the Marquis of Carabas.

"As you have observed, Sire," the Marquis replied; "property that never fails to yield plenty of revenue each year."

Master Puss, always running ahead, would say to any mowers he saw: "Good folk, if you do not say that all this wheat belongs to Monsieur, the Marquis of Carabas, I will have you minced up finer than a *pâté*."

Puss—always ahead of the coach—said the same thing to any he met; and the King was vastly impressed by the extensiveness of the property belonging to the Marquis.

Master Puss came at last to a splendid castle which was owned by an Ogre, the richest ever known; for everything the King had admired belonged to the Ogre. Puss had been at pains to find out who this Ogre was and how to behave to him. He had begged audience, he said, since one could not be in the vicinity of the castle without wishing to pay the Ogre homage.

The Ogre was equally polite—though an Ogre— and bade Puss be seated.

"I am told," said Puss, "that you are possessed of magic which enables you to change yourself into any kind of animal—a lion, for instance; an elephant . . ."

"True," the Ogre said brusquely, "and to prove it, you are going to see me turn into a lion."

Face to face with a lion, Puss was so terrified he was up on the roof in a flash, endangered as well since his boots were not safe for walking on tiles.

Presently, when the Ogre had taken back his shape, Puss climbed down, confessing that he had been badly frightened.

"They tell me too," he said, "but I couldn't believe it, that you can change yourself into one of the very tiniest animals—a rat or a mouse—which seems still more impossible."

"Impossible?" said the Ogre; "you shall see," and of a sudden a mouse was scampering over the floor.

Puss had no sooner seen it than he pounced on it and ate it.

The King, meanwhile, having noticed the Ogre's fine castle, wished to see the inside.

Puss, who had heard the sound of the coach on the drawbridge, ran to the King, exclaiming, "Welcome, Your Majesty, to the castle of Monsieur, the Marquis of Carabas"; the King inquiring, "Well! This castle is yours too, Marquis? Could anyone imagine a finer court or battlements? Might I have the pleasure of seeing the interior?"

The Marquis gave his hand to the young Princess, and following the King, who went first, they entered the banquet-hall, where a splendid collation was in readiness for friends of the Ogre, who were expected that day but had not dared to come in, knowing that the King was there.

The King, almost as charmed as his daughter by the graceful comportment of the Marquis of Carabas—his fancy dwelling on the splendid possessions of the Marquis—said, after accepting several little goblets of excellent wine, "Dear Marquis, why not—I really should like to have you as a son-in-law."

The Marquis, enraptured by his sudden felicity, and happier still to marry the beautiful Princess, acknowledged by a deep bow of acceptance the honor which the King had done him.

The wedding took place the same day.

Puss became a lord and, from then on, never ran after mice except for amusement.

The Sleeping Beauty

A king and queen, one time, had no child and were more despondent than anyone could say. They went to every known medicinal spring in the world and drank the waters, kept vows, undertook pilgrimages; every religious duty was performed in minutest detail; all useless. Finally the Queen was blessed by the birth of a little princess.

After the christening, the entire Court returned to the royal palace, where a magnificent reception honored the fairies, each place at table made resplendent by a magnificent setting—massive gold sword, spoon, fork, and knife of fine gold, encrusted with diamonds and rubies. But as each guest took her place, an old fairy appeared whom no one had invited because, being more than fifty years old and never having left her tumbledown tower, she was thought to be dead or enchanted. The King made a place for her but had no massive gold sword to give her, like those of the others, because only seven had been made for the seven fairies who had been invited. The old fairy, imagining that she was disdained, grumbled threats under her breath. A certain young fairy who was near and heard them then left the table and hid behind a tapestry, that she might speak last and undo, as far as possible, any harm the old fairy might try to do.

Meanwhile, grouping themselves about the cradle, the fairies began, one after the other, to speak the magic words which were to make of the babe the most accomplished princess in the world. The youngest ordained that she be the most beautiful person in the world. The next, that she should have the disposition of an angel; the third, that she should have the utmost grace in whatever she did; the fourth, that her dancing be perfection; the fifth, that she should sing like a nightingale; the sixth, that she should play skillfully on every kind of instrument. When the old fairy's turn came, bending over the cradle and shaking her head violently despite her great age, she ordained that the Princess should prick her finger on a spindle and die. This fearsome prophecy caused all who heard it to shudder; of those present there was not one who did not weep. At the same instant, the young fairy appeared from behind the tapestry and declared in ringing tones, "Take heart, Your Majesties, your daughter shall not die. True, I can not entirely undo the power of the witch's spell; the Princess will prick her finger on a spindle, but instead of dying, she will fall into a deep sleep which will last a hundred years, after which a king's son will come and waken her."

Attempting to evade the curse, the King issued a proclamation, making it unlawful, upon pain of death, for anyone to use a spindle.

In the summer, fifteen or sixteen years later, the King and Queen had gone to one of their country places and it chanced that the Princess, looking about here and there from dungeon to turret, stepped into a little attic where an old nurse was twirling her distaff. The good soul had lost her memory and no longer remembered that the King had forbidden anyone with a spindle to use it.

"What are you doing, good mother?" the Princess asked.

"Spinning, dear child," the old nurse, who did not recognize her, replied.

"Pretty!" the Princess answered. "How do you do it? Let me see if I can do it too?"

She had no sooner picked up the spindle—for she was impetuous, also heedless—than she pricked a finger and fainted. The old nurse, in distress, called for help, which came from all sides. They sprinkled water on forehead and face of the Princess, loosened her dress, chafed her hands, tried to restore circulation in her forehead with Hungarian water; nothing revived her. Then the King himself, who had run up the stair toward the sounds of commotion, recalled the witch's prediction and, realizing that what the fairy had foretold had befallen the Princess, had her laid on the finest bed in the palace on a coverlet embroidered with gold and silver—an angel you would have said, she was so beautiful, since fainting had in no way dimmed the tints in her cheek or the carmine of her lips. She had closed her eyes, that was all; but one could detect her gentle breathing—an assurance that she could not be dead.

The King decreed that she be allowed to sleep undisturbed until the hour had come when she was to wake. The good fairy who had saved her life by condemning her to sleep a hundred years was in the kingdom of Mataquin, twelve thousand leagues from where misfortune had befallen the Princess. Informed instantly, however, by a little dwarf with seven league boots which enabled him to span seven leagues at a stride, she set out at once and was seen arriving an hour later in a chariot of fire drawn by dragons. The King gave his hand to assist her descend from the car—she approving of all that he had done. But being an exceedingly provident fairy, she felt that the Princess on waking alone in the old palace, years later, would be perplexed. So she touched with her wand everyone in the palace except the reigning King and Queen: maids of honor, housemaids, men-in-waiting, officials, major-domos, cooks, kitchen helpers, cooks' assistants, errand boys, Swiss guards, pages, footmen. She touched every horse in the stables, and grooms, the big mastiffs kept in the inner court and the Princess's tiny lapdog beside her on the bed—that they should not wake any sooner than their mistress, so they might be ready to serve at her need; the partridges and pheasants, along with the twigs on the hearth— all asleep, the fire also: every needful thing done in a moment. Fairies were not slow workers.

Then the King and Queen kissed their child, having been careful not to wake her, left the palace and issued a proclamation making it a criminal offense to approach it, a precaution which was unnecessary since a quarter of an hour, say, had scarcely passed when trees, big and little, under-brush and sharp thorns had so interlaced themselves that neither man nor beast could have got through. Indeed nothing but the topmost towers of the castle could be seen even from a distance.

Beyond dispute, the fairy had done her utmost to ensure that while the Princess slept she could be in no danger of intrusion from the curious.

When the hundred years had passed, the son of the then reigning king (who of course had never heard of the Princess asleep in her castle surrounded by thorns), when out hunting one day, saw towers above the tree-tops of dense woods, and asked to whom they belonged. Each answered in his own way, one saying it was an old castle haunted by ghosts, others that witches held their orgies there. Nearly all supposed that an ogre lived there, who carried off any child he could catch, to devour at his whim, he alone being able to make his way through the dense wood.

The Prince did not know what to believe until an aged peasant spoke out and said, "My liege, more than fifty years ago, I heard my father say there was a princess in the castle, the most beautiful anyone had ever seen, that she was under a spell, must sleep a hundred years and that she would be awakened by a king's son whom she had been destined to wed."

On fire at the words, without stopping to think, the Prince resolved that he must afford the strange romance a conclusion; he must see what was there, and at once. He had scarcely taken a step when the great trees, brambles and thorns parted of themselves to let him through. He strode toward the castle, which he could see at the end of a long avenue, on further, entered and to his surprise saw that no one could follow—for as soon as he had passed, the trees came together again.

He pressed on. A prince, young and in love, is always brave, and this one, true to tradition, went boldly to the forecourt of the castle. There, what he saw would have frozen the blood of the bravest. In the fearsome silence, everything everywhere had the look of death—every creature prostrate— man and animal appeared lifeless. It was evident, however, by their regular breathing and the faces of the guards, that they were merely sleeping; their glasses, in which some drops were still left, verified that they had just been drinking when overtaken by sleep. The Prince crossed a wide, marble court, went up the stair and entered the guardroom, where he saw armed men, rank upon rank, rifle on shoulder, all fast asleep. He walked through room after room with footmen on duty and ladies-in-waiting; the first at attention, the others seated.

At length, he entered a room everywhere golden, where, with bed-curtains drawn back at each side, was the most beautiful thing he had ever seen—a princess of perhaps fifteen or sixteen, possessed of a splendor both of earth and of heaven. All admiration, he came forward atremble. Then the time having come for the enchantment to end, the Princess slowly opened her eyes, and gazing tenderly upon the Prince, the first thing on which her eyes could rest, she murmured, "Is it you, my Prince? How welcome!"

Then she smiled in a manner so loving that the Prince did not know what to say—charmed by her words and yet more by the way in which she said them, at a loss to express his joy and sense of blessedness. He loved her more, he said, than he mattered to himself. They talked about all sorts of things—shed some tears as well—less logical than fervent. That the Princess showed less confusion than the Prince is not surprising, since she had had time to dream of what she would say to him, for (although legend has not said so) it is permissible to infer that the good fairy—most provident of god-mothers—had provided her, during so long a sleep, with happy dreams. All in all, they talked four hours and had not yet said the half of what they had to say.

Meanwhile, the whole palace had come to life with the Princess. All, thinking of what had to be done and not in love, were dying of hunger, it being so long since they had had anything to eat.

The maid of honor, as impatient as the rest, announced to the Princess, in firm tones, that dinner was served. The Prince assisted the Princess to rise, magnificently and appropriately attired as she was, forbearing to tell her that it was in the style of her grandmother, with high Medici collar—in which she was none the less beautiful. They proceeded to the Hall of Mirrors and dined there, waited on by the staff of the Princess. Violins and hautboys performed old-time music—expertly even if it was a hundred years since they had played; and after dinner, losing no time, the palace chaplain married Prince and Princess in the chapel; whereupon the maid of honor drew the curtain, concluding events.

They scarcely slept, the Princess not yet much in need of sleep; and the Prince returned in the morning to the town, where the King, his father, was consumed with anxiety for his safety. The Prince told him that while hunting, because lost, he had had to sleep in the hut of a charcoal burner who had given him black bread and cheese to eat.

The King, his father, could be counted on to believe him, but his mother was not convinced, and in view of the fact that he spent nearly all his time hunting, and always made excuses for spending two or three nights away from home, was certain that he had a sweetheart—which was the case. For he lived with the Princess two entire years—in fact, had two children: the first, named Aurora, and a second—a son—whose name was Day, since he was even more beautiful than his sister. Many a time the Queen would try to draw him out about how he managed to pass the time, but he never risked confiding his secret. Although he loved her, he feared his mother, who was a descendant of ogres. (The King, indeed, would not have married her had it not been for her immense wealth.) Even at Court it was rumored that she had traits common to ogres—that it was all she could do, when she spied a small child, not to seize it like prey. So the Prince was not inclined to explain anything to her. But when the King died about two years later and the Prince succeeded to the throne, he made his marriage public and went to fetch his bride, who upon her entry into the town with her children, one on either side, was a magnificent sight.

Some time later the King, when at war with the Emperor Cant-a-butte, delegated authority to his mother, the Queen—urging that she send the young Queen and the children to their countryseat in the forest, that they might the better endure the consuming ennui they suffered. Presently she said to the proprietor of the lodge, in the tones of an ogress craving tender flesh, "I wish, for my dinner tomorrow, little Aurora."

"Ah, Madame!" said the man.

"I wish it," she said, "to eat with sauce *Robert.*"

The poor man, realizing that he must not disappoint an ogress, took his big knife and went up to the room of the little Aurora. She was four, and came skipping and laughing to throw her arms about him and beg bonbons. He wept; the knife fell from his hand and he went into the inner court to cut the throat of a little lamb, which he served with a sauce so fine, tke wicked Queen assured him she had never eaten anything so good. At the same time he carried little Aurora off and gave her to his wife to hide in a small room at the back of the inner court.

Eight days later, the wicked Queen said to the caretaker, "I wish, tomorrow, to eat little Day."

The man did not answer but resolved to deceive her as he had done the first time. He went to look for poor Day and found him with a little flower stalk in his hand, playing with a big monkey. He was still not more than three. The man took him to his wife, who hid him with little Aurora, and in his place served the Queen a bit of tender goat which she thought excellent.

All went well for a time, but one evening this wicked Queen said to the caretaker, "Tomorrow I wish the Queen for dinner, with the same sauce as the children."

This time the man despaired of deceiving her. The young Queen was twenty, not counting the hundred years she had slept. Her skin was a little tough, though beautiful and white, and by finding an animal of her age in a menagerie, the man resolved to do as he had done the second time. Not wishing to startle her, he told her of the order given him by the Queen.

"Do it, do it," she said, holding her neck out. "Carry out the command. I shall see my children again, my poor children whom I love so much"— she thinking them dead since they had been taken away without telling her anything.

"No, no, Madame," the good caretaker said, "you are not to die. You will see your dear children but it will be downstairs where I live. I am hiding them, and I shall deceive the Queen again, giving her a deer to eat in your place."

He led her as fast as he could to his quarters, where she could embrace her children and weep with them; then hastened to placate the Ogress with the deer, which she ate for supper with the same relish with which she would have eaten the young Queen, with no remorse for her cruelty, planning to tell the King on his return that ravenous wolves had devoured his wife and children.

One evening when she was prowling as usual through the courtyard of the castle to catch a scent of fresh meat, she heard little Day crying in an inner room; his mother, the Queen, was going to punish him because he had been naughty, and Aurora could be heard imploring pardon for her little brother.

The Ogress recognized the voices of mother and children and, enraged to have been deceived, decreed in a terrible voice that on the following morning a huge brazier should be set in the middle of the courtyard, that she might fill it with toads and vipers, snakes and other reptiles, then throw into it the Queen and her children. The caretaker, his wife and helpers were to have their hands tied behind them. Mother and children were just about to be thrown into the brazier by their tormentors when the King clattered into the courtyard on horseback— his return being so sudden, no one had expected him. Having come in haste—too overwhelmed to dismount—he commanded that not a soul proceed with the horrible pageant. The Ogress—the originator of it, foiled in venting her wrath—threw herself headfirst into the brazier, where she was immediately a victim of the loathsome creatures she had put there herself. It was distressing to the King that his mother should suffer, but mercifully he was to find consolation in his wife and children, each so dear to him—at last with him and able to comfort him.

Cinderella

One time a man whose wife had died married again,
and it was a woman with two daughters who were
as proud and disagreeable as she was herself, who
put on more airs than you ever saw—just like her
in everything. Now the man had a daughter of his
own who was as sweet and good as her mother had
been—with a nature nothing could match. The
wedding festivities were no sooner over than the
stepmother's ill will flared up; she could not bear
the sweet nature of the good child since the con-
trast made her daughters seem the more detestable.
She gave the worst tasks in the house to the good
one: scouring pans, scrubbing stairs, polishing
floors (my lady's own and the daughters' floor); had
her sleep in an attic on straw for a bed, whereas
the sisters had rooms with an inlaid floor and beds
in the latest style and tall mirrors in which they
could see themselves from head to foot. The poor

child endured it all patiently and did not complain to her father, who would have scolded her, because his wife ruled him completely. When the child had done her work, she would sit in the chimney corner in the ashes, and because of this they called her Cinderella. Even in her shabby dress, Cinderella was a hundred times prettier than her sisters, although their dresses were magnificent.

Then, as it happened, the King's son gave a ball to which he invited all persons of note, our sisters among the rest since they passed for great ladies thereabout. They were much gratified, and were busy every minute deciding which dresses to wear and what way of wearing their hair made them look best—which meant more hardship for Cinderella since it was she who did their linen and pleated their ruffles. They talked of nothing but how they should dress.

"I," said the elder, "shall wear my red velvet and rose-point bertha."

The younger said, "I have nothing better than what I have been wearing, but, to make up for it, can wear my capelet with the gold flowers and my set of diamonds—something you don't often see."

They needed an expert to dress their hair in double puffs and to buy the best patches, called Cinderella and asked her advice because she had good taste. She gave it—the best in the world, offering to dress their hair herself; and of this they were very glad. Then as she was giving their hair style, they said, "Cinderella, would you like to go to the ball?"

"Alas! You are making fun of me, ladies. It is out of the question," she said.

"True; if they saw you at the ball, they would laugh at a poor thing like you."

Anyone but Cinderella would have done their hair in a way that would have made them frights, but she was kindly and did it to perfection.

The sisters by this time were in such transports of joy, they went for nearly two days without eating, broke a dozen lacings to make their waists small, and were forever gazing at themselves in the mirror.

Finally the happy day had dawned; they went off to the ball and Cinderella followed them with her eyes as far as she could see them, then began to weep.

Her godmother, seeing her in tears, asked what was the trouble.

"I do wish . . . wish . . ."—then she gave way to sobs as if she would never stop.

Her godmother, who was a fairy, said, "You wish you were going to the ball, isn't that it?"

"Oh, dear. I do," Cinderella said with a sigh.

"Very well; be a good girl," her godmother answered. "I'll get you there; go into the garden and bring me a pumpkin."

Cinderella ran out instantly, cut the very finest pumpkin she could find and brought it to her godmother, not able to guess how the pumpkin could help her get to the ball.

Her godmother hollowed it out and, when nothing was left but the rind, tapped it with her wand and turned it into a beautiful coach, gilded all over. Then she looked into the mousetrap and found six live mice. She bade Cinderella open the door of the trap a little, and as each mouse came out, she touched it with her wand and it was changed into a beautiful horse—making three pairs of mouse-gray horses in harness.

Since a coachman was lacking, Cinderella said, "I'll go see if there isn't a rat in the trap to make a coachman."

"By all means," said her godmother, "go see."

Cinderella brought the rattrap back, in which there were three large rats. The fairy chose the one with the best whiskers, and when she had tapped him, he changed into a tall coachman with the finest whiskers ever seen.

That done, she said to her goddaughter, "Go into the garden; you will find six lizards back of the watering can; bring them to me."

Cinderella had no sooner brought them than her godmother changed them into six footmen who were instantly up behind the coach in chamois uniforms, sitting there rigid and real, as if they had never done anything else in their lives.

The fairy then said to Cinderella: "So now you can go to the ball. Aren't you happy?"

"Yes, but can I go as I am, in my dingy dress?"

Her godmother had merely to give a touch of her wand, and instantly the sorry rags turned to cloth of gold and silver. She also provided a pair of the very prettiest glass slippers in the world.

Thus attired, Cinderella stepped up into the coach; but her godmother impressed upon her, above all things, not to stay at the ball even a second after midnight or the coach would change back into a pumpkin; the horses, to mice; her footmen into lizards; and her clothes into rags. She promised her godmother that she would not fail to leave the ball before midnight, and drove away happy as could be.

The coach had no sooner entered the courtyard of the palace than the Prince was told that a very great princess had come, whom nobody knew. He ran to receive her, gave his hand to assist her descend from the coach, and led her to the ballroom.

Sudden silence fell; the dancing stopped, the violins ceased to play; everyone was breathless, admiring the beauty of this unknown guest. One heard nothing but mingled murmurs of: "Ah! What a beautiful person!"

The King himself could not take his eyes from her or stop whispering to the Queen that it was years since he had seen so lovely and lovable a person.

The ladies all fixed their eyes on her hair and ball gown, so that the next day they could be dressed in the same way, supposing they could find material as beautiful as hers and dressmakers skillful like hers.

The Prince led her to the place of honor, then gave her his hand for the dance. She danced so gracefully that everyone admired her the more.

Tempting refreshments were brought, of which the young Prince did not taste a morsel, he was so lost in admiration of his guest.

She seated herself by her sisters and was gracious to an extreme: gave them oranges and kumquats which the Prince had given her. What seemed more than strange was that they did not recognize her.

While they were conversing, she heard a quarter of twelve strike, made them all a deep bow and fled, hastening away as fast as she could.

On arriving home, she looked for her godmother and, after thanking her, said she would like to go to the ball the following evening, since the King's son had invited her.

As she was telling her godmother about all that had happened, the two sisters knocked at the door and Cinderella went to open it.

"How late you are," she said yawning, rubbing her eyes and stretching as if she had waked only then, although she had had no wish to sleep after they had left.

"If you had been at the ball," one of the sisters said, "you would have had no reason to yawn. The most beautiful princess appeared that you could ever have imagined. She was all courtesy and gave us oranges and kumquats."

Cinderella could not have been happier; she asked them the name of the Princess, but they could only say they did not know her and that the

King's son was beside himself, would give anything in the world to know who she was. Cinderella smiled and said, "She was such a beauty then? Oh, dear! You were fortunate. I could not ever see her? Oh, me! Miss Javotte, will you lend me your yellow dress that you wear every day?"

Javotte said coldly, "The idea! Lend my yellow dress to a cook's helper all over grease spots; I would be out of my mind."

Cinderella was expecting to be refused, for it would have been very embarrassing if her sister had been willing to lend the dress.

The next day both sisters attended the ball and Cinderella also—even more resplendent than the first time. The King's son was by her side all the time and never stopped telling of her charms. Young as she was, enjoying every minute, she forgot the warning her godmother had insisted upon; as a result, she heard the first stroke of midnight when she could not believe it was even eleven, rose, and was off as light as a deer. The Prince followed but could not overtake her. She sped away so fast that she lost one of her glass slippers. The Prince stooped reverently to pick it up and asked the palace guards if they had not seen a princess leave. They said they had seen no one go out but a young girl shabbily dressed, who looked more like a peasant than a young girl of fashion.

When her two sisters returned from the ball, Cinderella inquired if they had been delighted again, and if the beautiful guest had been there again. They said yes but that she had vanished at the stroke of twelve and with such speed that she had lost one of her little glass slippers—the prettiest ever. The King's son had picked it up, had done nothing but gaze at it the entire rest of the ball, and without a doubt had fallen hopelessly in love with the beautiful stranger to whom the slipper belonged.

Since they were right, a few days later it was proclaimed by heralds that the King's son would marry the person whose foot the slipper fitted exactly.

Immediately princesses, duchesses, and every Court lady competed in trying on the slipper, each doing her best to crowd a foot into it; but no one had a foot dainty and slender enough to get it on.

When the heralds arrived, that the sisters might try it on, Cinderella was watching, recognized her slipper, and said, smiling, "Might I see if it would not fit me?" The sisters began to laugh and make fun of her.

The young man who had been trying to find a foot to fit the slipper looked hard at Cinderella and, thinking her very beautiful, said it was true that he had been commissioned to request every young lady to try the slipper on; then asked Cinderella to sit down. He put the slipper on her shapely foot and saw that she had no trouble getting it on, that it fitted like a mould. The sisters were dumbfounded, but still more when Cinderella drew the other little slipper from her pocket and put it on her other foot. At that very moment her godmother appeared, who, when she had touched Cinderella with her wand, made her grander even than before. Then the two sisters recognized her as the beautiful guest they had seen at the ball and threw themselves at her feet, imploring pardon for all the bad treatment they had inflicted upon her. Cinderella helped them rise, embraced them, forgiving them with all her heart, asking that they love her from then on. She was escorted in her glittering dress to the young Prince, who thought her more beautiful than ever, and in a few days they were married.

Cinderella, who was as good as she was beautiful, had the two sisters come to live at the palace and found husbands for them in two nobles.